KIDS' SPORT STORIES

# TAE KWON DO TEST

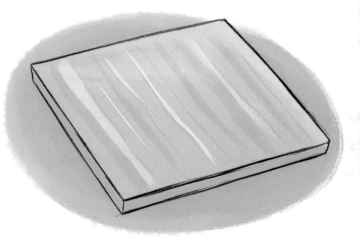

written by Cristina Oxtra

illustrated by Amanda Erb

raintree

a Capstone company — publishers for children

Raintree is an imprint of Capstone Global Library Limited, a company incorporated in England and Wales having its registered office at 264 Banbury Road, Oxford, OX2 7DY – Registered company number: 6695582

www.raintree.co.uk
myorders@raintree.co.uk

Designed by Ted Williams
Original illustrations © Capstone Global Library Limited 2020
Originated by Capstone Global Library Ltd
Printed and bound in India
982

978 1 4747 9374 2

**British Library Cataloguing in Publication Data**
A full catalogue record for this book is available from the British Library.

# CONTENTS

# Glossary

**ap chagi** front snap kick

**dolyo chagi** roundhouse kick

**kihap** shout

**poomse** forms in Tae Kwon Do; poomse are made of set patterns of movements

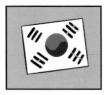

**Tae Kwon Do** Korean sport that began as self-defence and a way to train one's body and mind

## Chapter 1
# A GOOD PUPIL

Mina was learning a Korean sport called Tae Kwon Do. She wore a white belt with her uniform. White was for new pupils, just beginning to learn the sport. Mina dreamed of getting her yellow belt. She practised often and listened closely to her instructor.

"Mina, show me your front snap kick,"
said Master Yoon. "*Ap chagi.*"

Master Yoon held out a hand target.

Mina kicked the target ten times. She
shouted with each kick. "Heeyah!"

"Good kicks and loud *kihaps*," said Master Yoon.

"Thank you," Mina said.

"Now show me your roundhouse kicks," said Master Yoon. "*Dolyo chagi*."

Mina turned her body to one side. She kicked the target ten times. Again she shouted with each kick.

"Great," Master Yoon said. "Next, I'd like to see your *poomse*."

Mina moved her arms and legs the correct way.

Finally, Master Yoon held a soft foam board in front of Mina. Mina balled up her fist and hit the board hard.

"Heeyah!" Mina shouted.

"Well done!" said Master Yoon. "You are ready for your yellow belt test on Friday."

"Yes!" Mina said, a big smile on her face.

"During the test you will do everything you have shown me," Master Yoon said. "There will be one difference, though. You will hit a wooden board, not a foam board."

"I think I can do that," said Mina.

"I know you can," Master Yoon said.

"Stay focused and do your best. Give your maximum effort."

"Yes, I will," Mina said.

# Chapter 2
# TEST TROUBLES

After her lesson, Mina saw her friend Leo. The two of them had started Tae Kwon Do at the same time, but Leo's skills had developed more quickly than Mina's. He was bound to get his yellow belt soon.

"Leo, you're late. The lesson is over," Mina said.

"I'm here to watch my brother in the next lesson," said Leo. "My hand is still sore from my test last week."

"How did you hurt yourself?" Mina asked.

"I didn't hit the board properly the first time," Leo said.

"Oh. Did you try again?" said Mina.

"No. I should have kept trying, but I stopped," said Leo.

"I hope you come back to our lesson soon," Mina said.

Leo nodded. "I will. And I'll do the test again. I'm just not ready yet," he said.

Mina was quiet on the journey home.
Her parents asked her what was wrong.
She told them she did not want to take
the yellow belt test.

"Why? You've been practising and doing so well," her dad said.

Mina told them what happened to Leo. "I'm scared of hurting myself," she said. "Leo is so much better than I am. If he can't pass the test, I can't!"

"What did Master Yoon say about Friday's test?" her mum asked.

"She told me to stay focused and give my maximum effort," said Mina.

"Then take her advice, Mina," her dad said. "You can do it!"

# Chapter 3
# MINA TO THE MAX

Soon it was testing day. Mina stood at the edge of the mat with her parents. Tears filled her eyes.

"I don't want to do it," Mina said. "I can't."

"Yes, you can," her mum said with a hug.

Master Yoon called all the pupils. Mina's dad patted his daughter's shoulder. With wobbly legs, Mina stepped onto the mat. Testing began.

Mina punched with power. She kicked and shouted. "Heeyah!" she shouted over and over again. Every time she shouted, she felt better and stronger.

Her form was perfect. She moved her arms and legs correctly. Mina had almost finished. All she had left was the wooden board.

Mina stared at it. She thought about Leo and his hurt hand. Her stomach flipped. Her heart pounded. Sweat trickled down her face.

Mina turned to the crowd. Her parents
waved. Leo gave her a thumbs up.

Mina looked at the board again and took a deep breath. Then she shouted and hit the board with her fist.

The board didn't break.

Her hand wasn't sore, but Mina felt shaky. She wanted to stop.

The other pupils began to cheer.

"Come on, Mina!" they shouted.

Leo shouted, "Don't give up, Mina!"

Master Yoon said, "You can do it, Mina. Maximum effort, remember?"

Mina tightened her fist and raised it high over her head. With all of her strength and her loudest "HEEYAH!" she brought it down. *OOMPH!*

*CRACK!* The board split in two.

Everyone clapped and cheered. Mina

had passed her test!

At the belt ceremony later, Mina bowed and thanked Master Yoon. She took off her white belt. She watched her instructor tie the new one around her waist. Mina was no longer a beginner. She was now a proud yellow belt.

# MINA'S BANANA MILK

Mina celebrated her yellow belt with this popular Korean drink. Ask an adult to help you make it!

**You will need:**
- 1 ripe banana, peeled and sliced
- 350 millilitres milk
- 1 teaspoon honey
- ¼ teaspoon vanilla extract
- dash of nutmeg

Combine all ingredients in a blender. Blend until smooth.

# REPLAY IT

Take another look at this illustration. Mina had just failed to break the board on her first attempt. Master Yoon was ready for her to try again. How do you think Mina felt right then? What do you think she saw and heard before she hit the board again?

Now pretend you're Mina. Write a note to Leo to tell him how you felt before and after your second attempt.

# ABOUT THE AUTHOR

Cristina Oxtra is the author of *Stephen Hawking: Get to Know the Man Behind the Theory* and *Stan Lee: Get to Know the Comics Creator*. She has an MFA in creative writing for children and young adults from Hamline University, USA. Cristina and her son train and compete in Tae Kwon Do.

# ABOUT THE ILLUSTRATOR

Amanda Erb is an illustrator from the United States, currently living in Massachusetts, USA. She has a BFA in illustration from Ringling College of Art and Design. In her spare time, she enjoys playing football, learning Spanish and discovering new stories to read.